The Witness Who Disappeared

By

Richard Trillion Mantey

Table of Contents

Dedication

To every voice that has ever spoken the truth, even when it was difficult.

To those who stand up for justice, often without recognition.

And to the quiet courage of witnesses—known and unknown—whose words have helped bring light to places where darkness once lived.

May their stories remind us that truth, no matter how deeply hidden, always finds a way to be heard.

Acknowledgments

Every story is shaped not only by imagination but by the countless influences that inspire it.

I would like to express my deep appreciation to the many writers, investigators, journalists, and storytellers whose dedication to exploring truth and human complexity has influenced the spirit of this work. Their commitment to examining justice, memory, and human resilience continues to inspire readers and writers alike.

Special thanks also go to readers of mystery and psychological suspense—those who appreciate stories that challenge the mind while touching the heart. Your curiosity and passion for uncovering hidden truths make stories like this possible.

I am equally grateful to the friends, family members, and early readers who offered encouragement during the writing process. Their thoughtful feedback and support helped refine the narrative and deepen the emotional layers of the story.

Finally, my sincere gratitude goes to the broader community of readers who believe in the power of stories to illuminate difficult questions about truth, justice, and the human experience.

Every page of this book exists because stories matter—and because readers continue to seek meaning within them.

Chapter 1: The Last Testimony

A Night to Remember

The darkness enveloped the small town like a thick shroud, casting long shadows that seemed to whisper secrets of the past. On this particular night, the air was charged with an electric tension, as if the very atmosphere held its breath, anticipating the events that were about to unfold. A gathering of anxious townsfolk filled the local diner, their hushed voices blending with the clinking of coffee cups, each one yearning for news about the witness who had mysteriously vanished just days before the trial. Little did they know that this night would change everything, igniting a firestorm of intrigue and danger that would force them to confront their deepest fears and darkest truths.

As the clock ticked closer to midnight, Detective Layla Miller sat alone at a booth in the corner, her mind racing with the implications of the case. The disappearance of the key witness had thrown the impending trial into chaos, leaving the prosecution scrambling for answers. With each passing moment, the stakes grew higher, and Layla knew that time was not on her side. The witness had been the linchpin of the entire case, and without her testimony, a dangerous criminal might go free, potentially endangering the lives of many.

Suddenly, a loud crash shattered the tense atmosphere, drawing everyone's attention to the diner's entrance. A figure stumbled through the door, drenched in rain and panic-stricken. It was the witness, her eyes wide with fear as she scanned the crowd for safety. Gasps filled the room, and Sarah felt her heart race. This was the moment they had all been waiting for, but the look on the witness's face suggested that she had not escaped unscathed. The truth behind her disappearance was far more sinister than anyone could have imagined.

As the townsfolk rallied around the witness, questions erupted like wildfire. Where had she been? Who had taken her? And most importantly, what had she seen? The atmosphere shifted from relief to suspicion, as old grudges and hidden agendas began to surface. Layla realized that the town itself held secrets that intertwined with the witness's fate, and unraveling those secrets would be as dangerous as confronting the criminal they were trying to bring to justice.

With the night deepening around them, Layla vowed to uncover the truth, no matter the cost. The witness's return heralded a new chapter in the investigation, one that would lead to shocking revelations and high-stakes confrontations. As the clock struck midnight, it became clear that this was not just a night to remember; it was the beginning of a relentless pursuit of justice, where every decision could mean life or death, and every revelation could turn the town upside down.

The Disappearance

The small town of Maplewood had always been known for its tranquility, but that calm was shattered with the disappearance of key witness Victoria Lang. Just days before she was set to testify in a high-profile murder case, she vanished without a trace, leaving behind a community in shock and a police force scrambling for answers. Theories began to swirl, from abduction to voluntary disappearance, as investigators raced against time to uncover the truth. With every passing hour, the stakes grew higher, and the pressure on the police intensified.

Victoria was not just any witness; she was the linchpin in a case that had captured national attention. Her testimony could either convict a notorious criminal or set him free. The implications of her disappearance sent ripples through the legal system, raising questions about the effectiveness of witness protection programs and the lengths to which criminals would go to silence those who dare to speak out. As detectives delved deeper into Victoria's life, they uncovered a web of secrets that hinted at a far darker reality than anyone had expected.

Rumors began to circulate about Victoria's connections to unsavory characters, and her past began to unravel in unsettling ways. Friends and family were interviewed, but their accounts only deepened the mystery. Was Sarah a victim, or had she staged her own disappearance to escape a life she no longer wanted? Each lead seemed to lead to more questions than answers, leaving the investigators frustrated and the community anxious. As they explored the shadows of her life, the tension mounted, revealing chilling connections to local conspiracy theories that had long been dismissed as urban legends.

In the midst of this chaos, the courtroom drama escalated. The defense attorney seized the opportunity to undermine the prosecution's case, highlighting the absence of their key witness as a critical flaw. As the trial continued without Victoria, the stakes grew even higher for everyone involved. The pressure on law enforcement to locate her intensified, as did the public's fascination with her case. With every day that passed, the chances of finding her alive dwindled, leading to a race against time that felt increasingly desperate.

Ultimately, the investigation took an unexpected turn when new forensic evidence surfaced, reigniting hope among the detectives. This breakthrough not only altered the course of the investigation but also forced everyone to reconsider their assumptions about

Victoria's disappearance. As the truth began to unravel, it became clear that nothing in Maplewood was as it seemed, and the quest to find the missing witness would lead to shocking revelations that would change the town forever.

Chapter 2: Unraveling the Past

The Cold Case File

In the small town of Millfield, the cold case file lay undisturbed for years, gathering dust in the back of the police archives. It contained the haunting details of a missing person—Samantha Reed, a witness who vanished just days before she was set to testify in a high-profile court case. Her disappearance sent shockwaves through the community, raising questions about the safety of key witnesses and the lengths to which some would go to silence them. As investigators dug deeper into her life, they uncovered a web of secrets that suggested her disappearance was far from random.

Detective Scarlett Lawson was determined to breathe new life into the case, fueled by her own personal connection to Samantha. As she sifted through the old evidence, she found inconsistencies that hinted at a larger conspiracy. Witness statements contradicted each other, and the timeline of events leading to Samantha's disappearance seemed more like a puzzle than a straightforward investigation. With each piece of information, Sarah felt the pressure mounting—not just to solve the case, but to protect those who might still be at risk.

As Scarlett delved deeper into the investigation, she encountered a series of obstacles that seemed insurmountable. Key witnesses were reluctant to talk, fearful of the repercussions of revealing too much. The town, once a close-knit community, was now riddled with paranoia and mistrust. Scarlett's pursuit of the truth became a high-stakes game, where the wrong move could lead to dire consequences—not just for her, but for anyone connected to the case.

The investigation took a shocking turn when new forensic evidence surfaced, suggesting that Samantha may have been involved in something much darker than anyone had imagined. Digital footprints led to a hidden network of crime and technology, where missing persons were just the tip of the iceberg. As Scarlett connected the dots, she realized that Samantha's case was not an isolated incident but part of a larger pattern that could expose a chilling conspiracy reaching far beyond Millfield.

With the clock ticking and the stakes higher than ever, Scarlett raced against time to uncover the truth behind Samantha's disappearance. The once cold case was now a burning flame, igniting a passion within her to seek justice for the missing witness. As she prepared to confront the forces that had kept the truth hidden for so long, she knew that she was not just fighting for

Samantha, but for all those who had vanished without a trace, their stories waiting to be told.

A Small Town's Secrets

In the heart of a seemingly idyllic small town, whispers of hidden truths linger in the air like the scent of fresh-baked pie. The townsfolk, with their polite smiles and friendly nods, carry secrets that could shatter the quaint facade. Behind every door lies a story, and in this town, the most compelling tale is that of the witness who vanished without a trace. As investigators dig deeper, they discover that the roots of deception run deeper than they ever imagined.

The town's history is steeped in unsettling mysteries, with past crimes surfacing at the most inconvenient times. The locals, once eager to share their lives, suddenly become tight-lipped when discussions shift to the missing person cases that haunt their community. Rumors swirl like autumn leaves, hinting at conspiracies that stretch beyond the town limits. As the investigation unfolds, it becomes clear that the small-town charm is merely a mask for a much more sinister reality.

The psychological toll of the missing witness weighs heavily on everyone involved, from family members desperate for answers to law enforcement officials striving to untangle the web of lies. Each lead presents new challenges, as the pressure mounts to solve the case before it fades into obscurity. The stakes rise with every passing day, and the once-cozy streets transform into a labyrinth of fear and mistrust.

Technology plays a pivotal role in the search for the truth, as detectives employ forensic evidence to piece together the witness's last known movements. Surveillance footage, digital footprints, and social media clues become vital tools in unraveling the mystery. Yet, each discovery leads to more questions, revealing the depth of the town's secrets and the lengths to which people will go to protect their own.

Ultimately, the pursuit of the truth in this small town serves as a reminder that appearances can be deceiving. The disappearance of the witness not only exposes hidden agendas but also challenges the very fabric of community life. As the investigation reaches its climax, the revelations that come to light may not only bring justice for the missing but also change the town forever, leaving a lasting impact on its residents.

Chapter 3: The Witness Protection Program

A Life in Hiding

In the small town of Maplewood, the shadows held more secrets than the sunlit streets revealed. Within these shadows lived a woman named Abigail, who had once been a key witness in a high-profile murder case. After testifying against a notorious crime syndicate, she found herself thrust into a world of fear and anxiety, where every sound seemed amplified and every stranger a potential threat. Her life transformed overnight from that of a vibrant community member to a ghost haunting the very streets she once treaded freely.

Living in hiding was a complex web woven from paranoia and survival instincts. Abigail learned to navigate her new reality, where routine became a luxury she could no longer afford. Simple acts like grocery shopping or a visit to the park turned into elaborate missions filled with risks and calculated decisions. Each day was a test of her resolve, as she balanced the need for normalcy against the ever-present danger lurking just out of sight. Her heart raced at the slightest noise, a reminder of the consequences of her past choices.

The witness protection program promised safety, yet it came with a price. Abigail was forced to sever ties with her family and friends, living under a new identity that felt as foreign as the life she had left behind. The isolation began to wear on her, a constant reminder that the world outside was forever changed. She missed the simple joys of life, the laughter of friends, and the comfort of familiar faces. Each missed birthday and holiday only deepened the chasm of loneliness that threatened to consume her.

As time passed, the lines between past and present blurred. Flashbacks of her former life haunted her dreams, while the present became a haze of uncertainty. The fear of being discovered never waned, and the thought of the criminals she had betrayed haunted her waking hours. Sarah's mind became both her greatest ally and her worst enemy, constantly replaying the moments that led to her disappearance. In her quiet moments, she often wondered if the truth would ever come to light or if she would be lost forever in this self-imposed exile.

Amidst the turmoil, Abigail uncovered a new purpose. She began documenting her experiences, not only as a form of therapy but as an urgent reminder of the realities faced by those in witness protection. Her story, filled with twists and revelations, became a beacon for others who found themselves in similar predicaments. While she may never reclaim her old life, she discovered that her voice still held power, and perhaps, one day, she could step back into the light without the shadows following her.

The Choices We Make

In the heart of every investigation lies a series of choices that can turn the tide of justice. Each decision made by the key players—detectives, witnesses, and even the suspects—creates ripples that can lead to unexpected outcomes. The case of the missing witness exemplifies this truth; a single choice to speak or remain silent can shift the entire narrative. In a world where personal stakes are high and secrets are abundant, the choices we make become the threads that weave the complex tapestry of truth and deception.

Witness protection programs are designed to shield those who have seen too much, yet they often come with their own set of dilemmas. When a witness disappears, it raises alarming questions about loyalty, fear, and the lengths people will go to protect their identities. As investigators dig deeper into the mystery of the vanished witness, they unravel not only the facts of the case but also the moral implications of the choices surrounding it. The interplay of self-preservation and the pursuit of justice often leads to a psychological thriller that grips the reader.

Cold case investigations often hinge on the choices made years prior, choices that may have seemed innocuous at the time. A missed interview, a disregarded tip, or an overlooked piece of evidence can all contribute to a case growing cold. As detectives sift through the remnants of past decisions, they begin to understand that every choice has a consequence, and sometimes those consequences can haunt a community for decades. This adds depth to the narrative, compelling readers to ponder what could have been done differently.

In small towns, where everyone knows each other, the choices made can ripple through families and friendships like a stone thrown into a pond. When a key witness vanishes, the community is left to grapple with the fallout. Trust is tested, alliances are formed and broken, and the very fabric of social cohesion begins to fray. The stakes are raised as investigators not only seek the truth behind the disappearance but also navigate the intricate web of relationships that complicate their work.

Ultimately, "The Choices We Make" serves as a stark reminder that every decision, no matter how small, carries weight. In the labyrinth of crime and investigation, choices shape destinies, alter lives, and determine the course of justice. As readers journey through the twists and turns of this gripping narrative, they are invited to reflect on their own choices and the unseen consequences that may follow. In this world, the line between right and wrong is often blurred, and the choices we make can lead us to unexpected, and sometimes chilling, conclusions.

Chapter 4: Forensic Evidence

Clues from the Scene

In the quiet town of Maplewood, the scene of the crime was a chilling reminder of the night everything changed. Police tape fluttered in the early morning breeze, marking the perimeter around the abandoned warehouse where the witness had last been seen. The faint echo of sirens still lingered in the air, and detectives meticulously combed through every corner, seeking clues that could unravel the mystery of the missing witness. Each discarded item—a coffee cup, a torn piece of fabric—held the potential to tell a story that could lead them closer to the truth.

Amid the chaos, one crucial element stood out: the footprints in the dust. They were fresh, a stark contrast to the weathered floorboards that had been untouched for years. Analyzing the patterns, forensic experts deduced that the witness had likely been here just hours before their disappearance. This revelation sparked a myriad of questions. Who had they met? Was someone else involved? The detectives felt the weight of urgency pressing upon them, propelling their investigation deeper into the shadows of Maplewood.

As they explored the warehouse, they stumbled upon a hidden compartment behind a false wall. Inside lay a collection of documents that hinted at a larger conspiracy. Names and dates scribbled on yellowed pages suggested that the witness had uncovered something significant, something that could threaten powerful figures in the town. Each piece of evidence seemed to lead them further along a treacherous path, where the stakes were higher than they had ever anticipated.

The investigation took a sharp turn when they discovered a surveillance camera positioned nearby, its lens strategically aimed at the warehouse entrance. Reviewing the footage, they found a fleeting glimpse of the witness in conversation with a shadowy figure, just moments before the screen went dark. This sighting reignited hope among the detectives, fueling their determination to identify the figure and uncover what had transpired that fateful night.

As the dust settled and the pieces began to fall into place, it became evident that the clues from the scene were more than just remnants of a crime; they were the key to unlocking the truth behind the witness's disappearance. With each new lead, the detectives were drawn deeper into a web of deception, where trust was scarce and danger lurked at every corner. In a race against time, they had to decipher the meaning behind these clues, knowing that every moment counted in their pursuit of justice.

Technology in Crime Solving

In the age of advanced technology, crime solving has taken on a new dimension. Tools that once seemed like science fiction are now indispensable in the fight against crime. From DNA analysis to digital forensics, the integration of technology into investigations has revolutionized how detectives approach missing persons cases. This subchapter explores the pivotal role that technology plays in unraveling mysteries, particularly when key witnesses vanish without a trace.

One of the most significant advancements in crime solving is the ability to analyze forensic evidence with unprecedented precision. DNA profiling has become a cornerstone of modern investigations, allowing law enforcement to link suspects to crime scenes with a level of accuracy that was unimaginable just a few decades ago. In cases involving missing persons, this technology can provide crucial leads, transforming cold cases into solvable mysteries. The ability to extract DNA from even the smallest samples can lead to breakthroughs that bring long-awaited closure to families.

Digital forensics has also emerged as a vital component in contemporary investigations. The digital footprints left by individuals can reveal a wealth of information. From social media activity to mobile phone records, detectives can piece together the last movements and communications of a missing person. This evidence can not only help locate the individual but can also shed light on potential suspects or motives. As technology evolves, the methods of obtaining and analyzing digital evidence continue to expand, paving the way for more effective crime-solving strategies.

Moreover, surveillance technology has become increasingly sophisticated, providing law enforcement with valuable resources in real-time. The proliferation of CCTV cameras in public spaces means that investigators can trace the movements of both victims and suspects with ease. In the context of a missing persons case, these visual records can be crucial in establishing timelines and identifying potential witness accounts. As cities become more interconnected, the role of surveillance in crime solving will only grow, raising important ethical questions about privacy and monitoring.

Finally, the application of artificial intelligence and machine learning in crime investigations is on the rise. These technologies can analyze vast amounts of data to identify patterns and predict future criminal behavior. By harnessing the power of AI, law enforcement agencies can optimize their resources and enhance their investigative processes. As the landscape of crime changes, integrating technology into crime solving will be essential for staying one step ahead of those who seek to exploit vulnerabilities, especially in high-stakes cases involving witnesses who disappear without a trace.

Chapter 5: The Investigation Begins

Reopening Old Wounds

As the investigation into the chilling disappearance of the key witness unfolded, emotions ran high. The small town, once a quiet backdrop, transformed into a hotbed of rumors and suspicions. With every passing day, the pressure mounted on law enforcement to uncover the truth behind the vanishing act, dragging old wounds to the surface. Each person interviewed seemed to hold a piece of the puzzle, yet no one could provide a clear picture of what happened that fateful night.

Detective Olivia Jensen found herself entangled in not just the case, but also the town's complex web of secrets. Long-buried grudges and unresolved conflicts resurfaced as she dug deeper, revealing a community not as innocent as it appeared. The witness's disappearance was not merely about a missing person; it was a catalyst that forced the town to confront its dark past. Each lead brought with it a haunting reminder of betrayal and loss, pushing Olivia to question her own judgment about the people she thought she knew.

The forensic evidence collected from the scene painted a grim narrative, but it was the psychological aspects of the case that intrigued Sarah the most. The mind games played by those involved twisted the investigation into a labyrinth of deception. As she pieced together the witness's last known movements, it became clear that the truth was buried beneath layers of fear and manipulation. The more she learned, the more she realized that uncovering the truth would require not just skill, but an unwavering resolve to confront the town's demons.

As old wounds reopened, the emotional toll became evident on everyone involved. Families that had been torn apart by past actions were forced to reckon with their history, and friendships that seemed unbreakable began to fracture. Olivia understood that the resolution of this case would not only hinge on finding the witness but also on healing the scars inflicted on the community. Each interaction was charged with tension, as past grievances intertwined with the urgency of the present, creating a volatile atmosphere ripe for explosive revelations.

In a race against time,Olivia faced the daunting challenge of unraveling a conspiracy that reached beyond the town's borders. The stakes were higher than ever, with not just the witness's life on the line, but also the very fabric of the community. As she gathered the final pieces of the puzzle, the realization dawned that the truth could either restore faith in justice or further fragment the town's fragile unity. The reopening of these old wounds was not just a journey into the past; it was a harrowing exploration of what it means to seek justice in a world where the lines between right and wrong are often blurred.

The Police Involvement

The involvement of the police in the case of the vanished witness was both pivotal and perplexing. As the investigation unfolded, officers faced the daunting task of piecing together fragmented clues left behind. Each piece seemed to lead nowhere, complicating their efforts to find the one individual who held the key to solving a high-profile case. The pressure mounted, not only from the families of the missing but also from the media, demanding answers and quick resolutions. This created an atmosphere of urgency that hung heavily over the precinct.

Detective Isabella Mitchell had been assigned to the case, her reputation as a steadfast investigator preceding her. She understood the stakes involved; the witness was not just missing, but their disappearance threatened to unravel a tightly woven narrative that had already begun to sway public opinion. With every passing day, the urgency intensified as leads grew cold. Isabella's instincts told her that the answer lay hidden among the small town's secrets, and she was determined to uncover them, despite the obstacles.

As the police delved deeper into the investigation, they uncovered layers of conspiracy that hinted at far more than just a simple disappearance. The witness had been involved in sensitive information that implicated key players in the community. This revelation sent shockwaves through the department, and the once straightforward case transformed into a complex web of deceit. Isabella knew that to solve this mystery, she would need not only to follow the evidence but also to navigate the murky waters of trust and betrayal.

With the pressure mounting, Sarah found herself at the center of scrutiny. The media painted the police as ineffective, clamoring for a resolution that seemed increasingly elusive. Each day without progress fed into the narrative of failure, and the pressure from her superiors was palpable. Yet, she remained focused, knowing that emotional responses could cloud judgment. Her determination to find the witness was unwavering, driven by a sense of justice that demanded closure for those left in the wake of the disappearance.

Ultimately, the police involvement in this case was a testament to the challenges law enforcement faces when dealing with missing persons. The intersection of technology, forensic evidence, and psychological profiling became critical tools in Isabella's arsenal.

As she continued her search, she realized that sometimes, the truth lies in the shadows, waiting for someone brave enough to bring it to light. The road ahead was fraught with twists and turns, but she was committed to uncovering what truly happened to the witness who vanished into thin air.

Chapter 6: Shadows of Doubt

The Suspects Emerge

As the investigation into the disappearance of the key witness progressed, several suspects began to emerge, each with their own motives and secrets. The small town, once a serene backdrop, now buzzed with whispers and suspicion. Detective Sarah Mitchell felt the weight of the case pressing down on her as she delved into the lives of those connected to the witness. She knew that in a town where everyone thought they knew everyone else, the truth could be more elusive than ever.

Among the suspects was the victim's estranged brother, who had a history of conflict with the witness. His unpredictable temper and recent financial troubles painted a troubling picture. Eyewitness accounts suggested he had been seen near the location where the witness vanished. But was he truly capable of foul play, or was he just an unfortunate scapegoat in a web of deceit?

Then there was the enigmatic neighbor, a reclusive figure who had always seemed a bit too interested in the goings-on of the witness. With an extensive background in technology, he had the means to manipulate evidence and create alibis. Detective Mitchell couldn't shake the feeling that his silence masked a deeper knowledge of the case. Each interaction with him left her questioning whether he was a mere observer or a key player in the witness's disappearance.

As the investigation unfolded, a disturbing pattern began to materialize. Connections between the suspects hinted at an intricate conspiracy, far beyond a simple missing persons case. The deeper Sarah dug, the more she uncovered a network of small-town secrets intertwined with dark motives. The implications were staggering; this was no ordinary case, and the stakes were rapidly escalating.

With every new lead, the tension in the town amplified. Friends turned against each other, and alliances formed in the shadows. The key witness who had vanished was more than just a victim; their disappearance was the catalyst that threatened to unravel the fabric of the community. Detective Mitchell had to navigate through layers of deception and danger, knowing that the truth was not just vital for the case, but for the very survival of those still left in the town.

Psychological Profiling

Psychological profiling is a crucial component in unraveling the mysteries surrounding missing persons cases. It allows investigators to delve into the minds of both victims and perpetrators, providing insights that can guide the investigation.

By understanding the psychological makeup of individuals involved, law enforcement can develop more effective strategies for locating missing witnesses and understanding the motivations behind their disappearances.

In many cases, the profile of a missing person highlights their behavioral patterns, relationships, and potential vulnerabilities that may have led to their vanishing. For instance, examining the circumstances leading up to the disappearance can reveal critical clues about the individual's state of mind. Was the person under stress? Were there recent changes in their life that could have influenced their decision to disappear? These questions form the backbone of the psychological analysis conducted by investigators.

Moreover, psychological profiling extends beyond the victims to include potential suspects. Understanding the psychological triggers that might lead someone to commit a crime is essential in building a comprehensive case. Profilers analyze past behaviors, personality traits, and even socio-economic backgrounds to create a profile that can help narrow down suspects and predict their next moves. This aspect of psychological profiling is particularly vital in high-stakes investigations where every detail can mean the difference between success and failure.

Additionally, the role of modern technology in psychological profiling cannot be overlooked. With advancements in data analysis and forensic psychology, investigators can now utilize sophisticated tools to enhance their profiling techniques. These technological innovations allow for the analysis of vast amounts of information, drawing connections that might not be immediately apparent. As a result, psychological profiling has become an indispensable tool in contemporary criminal investigations, particularly in complex cases involving missing persons.

Ultimately, psychological profiling serves as a bridge between the known and the unknown, guiding investigators through the murky waters of human behavior. It emphasizes the importance of understanding the psychological aspects behind a disappearance while also shedding light on the larger narratives at play, such as societal pressures and individual struggles. In "The Witness Who Disappeared," this intricate web of psychological insights adds depth to the narrative, making it a compelling read for thriller enthusiasts who crave both mystery and psychological intricacies.

Chapter 7: High-Stakes Twists

Unexpected Revelations

The quiet town of Maplewood was never the same after the disappearance of key witness, Lisa Grant. Once an active participant in the community, her sudden absence sent shockwaves through the local police department and the families involved in the case she was set to testify in. Rumors swirled about what could have possibly happened to her, igniting a wildfire of theories that ranged from conspiracy to foul play. As investigators delved deeper, they unearthed a tangled web of secrets that suggested Lisa's life was far more complicated than anyone had realized.

As the investigation progressed, unexpected revelations began to surface. Friends and family members who once painted a picture of a straightforward life started revealing hidden connections to dubious characters and shadowy dealings. It became clear that Lisa had been involved in something much larger than a simple witness testimony. The closer they looked, the more entangled her life appeared, filled with cryptic messages and clandestine meetings that hinted at a conspiracy lurking just beneath the surface of Maplewood's idyllic facade.

Detective Evelyn Mills, leading the investigation, found herself grappling with the psychological implications of Lisa's disappearance. Each new piece of evidence seemed to unravel another layer of deceit, leading her to question the motives of those closest to Lisa. The pressure mounted as the clock ticked down to the trial, and Sarah knew that without Lisa's testimony, the case would likely collapse. The stakes were high, and the tension in the town escalated as fear and paranoia took hold.

In a twist that no one saw coming, a cryptic note was discovered hidden beneath Lisa's floorboards, stirring the investigation into a frenzy. The note revealed connections to a broader network that extended well beyond Maplewood, hinting at a conspiracy that involved law enforcement officials and powerful figures in the town. This shocking turn of events forced Evelyn to confront the uncomfortable reality that the very people tasked with protecting the community may be complicit in a cover-up.

As the case unfolded, the community was forced to confront its own demons, questioning who could be trusted and what secrets lay buried in their midst. The unexpected revelations not only changed the course of the investigation but also exposed the intricate ties that bound the residents of Maplewood together. With the truth on the line, the race was on to find Lisa before the trial commenced, knowing that her return may be the only hope for justice in a town riddled with deception.

The Race Against Time

As the clock ticked down, Detective Grace Thompson felt the pressure mounting. The case of the missing witness had spiraled into a frantic race against time. With each passing hour, the likelihood of finding him diminished, and the stakes escalated. Not only was the witness crucial for the upcoming trial, but his disappearance also hinted at a larger conspiracy that could unravel the very fabric of their small town.

The investigation took Grace through a labyrinth of secrets. She interviewed friends, family, and acquaintances, piecing together fragments of information that painted a picture of a man haunted by his choices. Each lead led to more questions, and the deeper she dug, the more she uncovered about the dark underbelly of the community. It became evident that someone wanted this witness silenced, and the urgency of the case was palpable.

Meanwhile, the courtroom loomed ominously on the horizon. The trial date was set, and without the witness's testimony, justice for the victim seemed unattainable. Grace knew that time was not just a factor; it was the enemy. She collaborated with forensic experts and utilized cutting-edge technology to trace digital footprints, hoping to uncover clues that could lead to the witness's whereabouts before it was too late.

As the investigation intensified, Grace found herself racing against not just time, but also unseen adversaries. The threats became increasingly tangible, and she realized that her own safety was at risk. The pressure of the case weighed heavily on her shoulders, and she grappled with the fear of failing to protect not only the missing witness but also the very integrity of the justice system.

In a gripping climax, the final moments of the countdown approached. With a breakthrough that could change everything, Grace was faced with a choice that would test her morals and resolve. The truth she sought was tantalizingly close, but would it come at a cost? In this race against time, every decision mattered, and the resolution of the case hung in the balance, poised to either shatter lives or restore hope for justice.

Chapter 8: Conspiracy Theories

Whispers in the Dark

In the small town of Maplewood, shadows danced under the flickering streetlights, concealing secrets that had long been buried. The disappearance of key witness Sarah Mitchell sent shockwaves through the community, igniting a frantic investigation that revealed dark undercurrents of deceit and desperation. As the police scoured the area for clues, whispers of conspiracy began to swirl, suggesting that Sarah's vanishing act was no mere coincidence but a calculated move to protect someone—or something.

Detective Mark Reynolds, a seasoned investigator with a reputation for solving the toughest cases, was assigned to unravel the mystery. He quickly discovered that Stella was not just a witness; she held the key to a web of corruption involving influential figures in the town. Each lead he followed seemed to vanish like smoke, and soon it became clear that the truth was being actively suppressed. With every tick of the clock, the stakes rose higher, pushing Reynolds to the edge as he faced threats that lurked in the shadows.

As Reynolds delved deeper into Stella's life, he uncovered a trail of hidden relationships and buried secrets. The more he learned about her connections, the more he realized that the people closest to her might not be who they seemed. Friends turned into suspects, and the lines between right and wrong blurred. With time running out, Reynolds had to navigate a treacherous landscape where loyalty could be a mask for betrayal, and allies might be working against him.

Tension escalated when Reynolds received an anonymous tip leading him to an abandoned warehouse on the outskirts of town. The air was thick with anticipation as he approached the dimly lit entrance, heart pounding. Inside, he found evidence that pointed to a larger conspiracy, one that implicated powerful members of the community. The realization hit him hard: Stella's disappearance was a warning, and if he wasn't careful, he could be next.

In a race against time, Reynolds had to piece together the clues before the darkness consumed him. As he confronted those who had a vested interest in keeping the truth hidden, he realized that trust was a luxury he could no longer afford. Whispers in the dark became a constant reminder of the stakes involved, and he understood that in this game of cat and mouse, the only way to bring Stella back and expose the conspiracy was to step into the shadows himself, where the real danger awaited.

Connecting the Dots

In the heart of the small town of Maplewood, whispers filled the air as the investigation into the disappearance of key witness Sarah Langley intensified. Her sudden vanishing left more questions than answers, igniting a firestorm of intrigue that gripped the community. As detectives pieced together the fragmented clues, they uncovered a web of secrets that intertwined the lives of residents in ways they never imagined. Each person had a story, but only Lily held the key to unraveling the truth behind a chilling crime that rocked the town.

Detective Mark Sullivan, a seasoned investigator with a keen sense for detail, found himself at the center of the storm. With mounting pressure from both the media and the police department, he knew that connecting the dots was crucial. Every lead pointed towards a broader conspiracy, one that threatened to silence anyone who dared to expose it. As he delved deeper into Lily's life, he discovered her involvement in a witness protection program, a revelation that complicated the case and raised the stakes significantly.

Meanwhile, Lily's family grappled with their own demons, struggling to cope with the uncertainty of her fate. Her sister, Emily, refused to accept the possibility that Lily was gone forever. Driven by love and determination, she initiated her own investigation, reaching out to friends and acquaintances to seek answers. Emily's relentless pursuit of the truth mirrored the detective's efforts, as both were unwittingly drawn into a dangerous game of cat and mouse with those who wanted Lily's silence.

As the investigation unfolded, the townsfolk began to realize that their peaceful existence was built on a foundation of lies. Hidden agendas and long-buried grudges surfaced, leading to shocking revelations about the very fabric of their community. The deeper they dug, the more perilous the journey became, as the truth about Sarah's disappearance threatened to expose the darkest corners of Maplewood. With every twist and turn, the tension escalated, leaving everyone questioning whom they could truly trust.

In a race against time, Detective Sullivan and Emily formed an unlikely alliance, uniting their efforts to find Lily before it was too late. As they navigated through a labyrinth of deceit, they uncovered a sinister plan that linked Lily's disappearance to a larger network of criminal activity. With the clock ticking, they knew that the only way to bring Lily home was to confront the ghosts of the past and reveal the shocking connections that bound them all together. In the end, the truth would not only change their lives but could potentially save them from the clutches of an unseen enemy.

Chapter 9: The Town's Response

Community Reactions

The small town of Millfield was shaken to its core when the news spread about the mysterious disappearance of a key witness in a high-profile murder case. Residents, who had always felt a sense of security in their close-knit community, found themselves grappling with fear and uncertainty. Conversations in cafes and on front porches turned to speculation and worry, as people wondered how someone could vanish without a trace. The local police were under immense pressure to find answers, fueling a growing tension that hung in the air like a storm cloud.

Secrets Revealed

In the heart of the investigation, secrets began to unravel like a tightly wound ball of yarn. The missing witness, a seemingly ordinary man named Thomas, had vanished without a trace, leaving behind a trail of unanswered questions. As detectives combed through his life, they discovered layers of deception intertwined with his existence. What had Thomas seen that compelled him to disappear? The deeper they dug, the more the pieces of the puzzle began to fit together, revealing a world where trust was a luxury few could afford.

Amidst the frantic search, whispers of a conspiracy emerged, hinting at connections that stretched far beyond the small town. The police uncovered hidden connections between Thomas and a powerful figure, raising the stakes of the investigation. This was no longer just about a missing person; it was a race against time to expose the truth that someone was desperate to keep buried. As the tension mounted, the detectives realized that every clue brought them closer to a danger they hadn't anticipated.

In a shocking turn of events, an old friend of Thomas resurfaced, providing a crucial lead that sent the investigation spiraling. This friend revealed that Thomas had been involved in a witness protection program, suggesting that his disappearance was orchestrated by forces beyond their control. The revelation sent ripples through the police department, igniting a fervor to uncover the details kept hidden for so long. Was Thomas truly in danger, or was he complicit in a game much larger than anyone had imagined?

As the clock ticked down, the detectives faced mounting pressure from both the media and the victim's family. The stakes were not just about finding Thomas but also about the integrity of the justice system itself. With each passing day, the possibility of finding him alive diminished. The investigation became a race against time, culminating in a high-stakes confrontation that would either open the floodgates to the truth or seal Thomas's fate forever.

In the end, the secrets revealed were not just about the missing witness but also about the lengths people would go to protect their own. As the dust settled, the ramifications of the investigation echoed through the town, leaving a lasting impact on its residents. The story of Thomas served as a stark reminder that in a world rife with conspiracy and deception, the truth often lies just beneath the surface, waiting to be uncovered in the most unexpected of ways.

Chapter 10: The Truth Uncovered

Final Clues

As the investigation progressed, the detectives found themselves sifting through a web of lies and half-truths. Every lead seemed to circle back to the same elusive figure, the missing witness whose testimony could unravel the entire case. With each passing day, the urgency mounted, as they raced against time to find the one person who held the key to justice. The pressure was palpable, and the stakes had never been higher.

In a small town where secrets were currency, everyone had something to hide. The detectives interviewed neighbors, family members, and even the local shopkeepers, but the witness's disappearance cast a long shadow over their efforts. Whispers of conspiracy began to surface, and the team realized that this was not just a simple missing persons case. It was a tangled mess of motives, where the truth was buried deeper than they had anticipated.

Meanwhile, forensic evidence began to paint a clearer picture. An analysis of the witness's last known whereabouts revealed inconsistencies in the timelines provided by those around her. The detectives had to follow these breadcrumbs, piecing together a story that seemed to shift with every new revelation. Each clue brought them closer to understanding not only what had happened but also who might have wanted to silence the witness for good.

As they delved deeper, they uncovered connections to a witness protection program that had been compromised. This shocking twist introduced a new layer of complexity to the case and raised questions about the integrity of those involved. The detectives faced a daunting challenge: how to navigate the murky waters of protection and betrayal while keeping their investigation on track.

In the final moments of their search, a breakthrough connected the witness to a chilling conspiracy that extended far beyond their small town. With time running out, they raced to piece together the final clues, knowing that a single misstep could lead to a catastrophic end. In a world where nothing was as it seemed, the truth was the only thing that could save them all.

Justice Served

In the small town of Willow Creek, the disappearance of key witness Ava Mitchell sent shockwaves through the community. As the trial for the notorious crime boss proceeded without her testimony, the atmosphere grew tense. With high stakes and lives hanging in the balance, the pressure mounted on the local police to find her. They delved into every lead, yet Ava seemed to have vanished without a trace. The townspeople whispered about her fate, fueling rumors of conspiracy and betrayal lurking beneath the town's surface.

Detective Mark Jensen, a seasoned investigator with a knack for solving cold cases, took it upon himself to unravel the mystery. As he combed through evidence, he uncovered a web of secrets that pointed to a well-planned disappearance. Witness protection programs and shady alliances came into the picture, complicating the case further. Each new piece of information led to more questions, and Mark realized that the answers could be dangerous. The closer he got to the truth, the more perilous his journey became.

The courtroom drama intensified as Ava's absence became a focal point in the trial. The defense attorney capitalized on her disappearance, arguing that the prosecution's case was built on shaky ground without her account. The tension was palpable, with jurors visibly anxious and the public on edge. Mark knew that time was running out; he had to locate Ava before the trial reached its climax. The stakes were higher than ever, and he felt the weight of responsibility on his shoulders.

As days turned into weeks, a breakthrough came when a tip-off led Mark to an abandoned cabin on the outskirts of town. Inside, he found evidence that suggested Ava had been there recently. The remnants of a struggle, coupled with her personal belongings, painted a grim picture. It became clear that she had been silenced, but by whom? The implications of this discovery sent chills down Mark's spine, awakening a fierce determination to bring justice to light.

With the trial looming and the clock ticking, Mark raced against time to piece together the puzzle. He confronted shadows from the past and unearthed connections that linked powerful figures to Ava's disappearance. As he prepared to reveal his findings in court, he knew that the truth would not only serve justice but also unearth the dark secrets of Willow Creek. The day of reckoning was approaching, and it would either mark the end of a sinister conspiracy or leave the town forever shrouded in mystery.

Chapter 11: The Aftermath

Lives Changed Forever

In a small town where everyone thought they knew each other, the sudden disappearance of a key witness sent shockwaves through the community. The case had seemed straightforward, but with the witness gone, the investigation took a dark turn. Friends turned to suspects, secrets were unearthed, and trust began to erode. Those who once shared laughter now whispered in hushed tones, wondering what could have happened to someone they thought they knew so well.

As the authorities scrambled to piece together the timeline, the lives of the townsfolk began to unravel. Families were torn apart by suspicion, and the very fabric of their small community was tested. The missing witness was not just a key figure in a courtroom drama; they were a friend, a neighbor, and a beloved member of the town. The emotional toll was palpable as people grappled with the harsh reality that someone they cared about might never return.

Amidst the chaos, the investigation revealed layers of deception and betrayal that had been lurking beneath the surface. Old grudges and hidden agendas came to light, complicating the search for the truth. Friends became enemies, and the line between loyalty and self-preservation blurred. Each revelation was a reminder that the witness's disappearance was more than a case; it was a catalyst that forever changed the lives of those left behind.

The courtroom became a battleground where the stakes were not just about justice but also about redemption. Every testimony, every piece of evidence, held the potential to alter lives irrevocably. The pressure mounted as the community awaited answers, and the realization dawned that not only was the witness lost, but so were the dreams and futures of many who had been touched by this tragedy.

As the dust settled, the aftermath of the case left an indelible mark on the town. Some sought closure, while others were haunted by unanswered questions. The lives changed forever were a testament to the fragility of trust and the profound impact of a single event. The missing witness may have vanished, but their absence echoed through the lives of everyone who remained, reminding them that sometimes, the true mysteries are found in the hearts of those left behind.

Moving Forward

In the aftermath of the tumultuous events that led to the disappearance of the key witness, the investigation takes a new direction. The small town, once vibrant with life, now feels shrouded in secrets and whispers. As the authorities sift through the clues left behind, they begin to uncover a web of deceit that stretches far beyond what anyone could have imagined. Each piece of evidence brings with it not just a potential lead but also a fresh wave of tension among the townsfolk, who are torn between their desire for the truth and their fear of the implications it might bring.

The protagonist, a determined investigator, finds herself at a crossroads. With every passing day, the pressure mounts to solve the case before it slips into oblivion. As she delves deeper into the witness's past, she discovers connections to a conspiracy that could shake the town to its core. The lines between ally and enemy blur, and she realizes that not everyone wants the truth to come out. Trust becomes a rare commodity, and she must navigate through layers of betrayal to piece together the mystery.

As the investigation intensifies, the stakes rise significantly. With the clock ticking, the investigator's resolve is tested, pushing her to confront not only the external threats but also her internal doubts. The haunting question of what happened to the witness looms large, compelling her to take risks that could jeopardize her career and her safety. Every new lead is a double-edged sword, revealing the fragility of the human psyche when faced with the unknown.

Amidst the chaos, the story shifts to the perspective of the vanished witness, whose journey unfolds in parallel. Captivity, fear, and a desperate fight for survival illuminate the psychological turmoil that accompanies such a disappearance. The witness's struggle to find hope while navigating a landscape of betrayal serves as a poignant reminder of the human spirit's resilience. This dual narrative enriches the mystery, creating a tapestry of suspense that keeps the reader guessing until the very end.

As the climax approaches, the investigator races against time, piecing together the last fragments of the puzzle. The resolution promises not only to unveil the truth behind the witness's disappearance but also to challenge the very foundations of the community's trust. In a world where nothing is as it seems, the final revelations will force the characters—and the readers—to confront their own beliefs about justice, loyalty, and the cost of uncovering the truth. The journey forward is fraught with danger, but it is also a testament to the indomitable will to seek justice, no matter the personal cost.

Chapter 12: Reflections on Witnesses

The Cost of Silence

In the heart of every investigation lies a truth that can shatter lives and reveal the darkest corners of human nature. "The Cost of Silence" delves into the unsettling reality of those who choose to remain mute in the face of evidence and the consequences that follow. Silence can be a powerful weapon, often wielded by those who fear the repercussions of speaking out. In a world where the missing are desperate for answers, the unwillingness to share knowledge can be as dangerous as the act of disappearance itself.

As the clock ticks down on a missing persons case, the stakes rise dramatically. Each passing hour intensifies the urgency, drawing in investigators who are driven not only by duty but by a deeply personal need for resolution. Yet, amidst the search parties and police tapes, there are whispers of secrets, a silent agreement among witnesses to remain quiet. These moments of hesitation can transform a simple inquiry into a labyrinth of deception, where every choice to stay silent can lead to irreversible outcomes.

The psychological toll of silence is profound, affecting both the witnesses and the families of the missing. Those who hold back information often grapple with guilt and fear, fearing the repercussions that may follow if they speak out. In small towns, where everyone knows each other, the weight of community expectations can stifle the truth. The emotional burden of knowing something yet choosing not to share can lead to a spiraling spiral of anxiety and regret, ultimately complicating the quest for justice.

In this exploration, we also examine the role of technology in unraveling the threads of silence. Forensic evidence and digital footprints can serve as powerful tools to break through barriers of communication. Investigators harness technology to piece together fragmented stories, revealing the hidden narratives that silence attempts to conceal. As the narrative unfolds, it becomes clear that silence is not merely a lack of speech; it is a complex interplay of fear, loyalty, and the human condition.

Ultimately, "The Cost of Silence" serves as a haunting reminder that every choice comes with a price. In the world of crime and investigation, the decision to remain silent can lead to devastating consequences, not just for the missing, but for the witnesses themselves. Their stories intertwine, revealing a tapestry of hidden truths that, if spoken, could alter the course of justice and restore hope to those who have long suffered in silence.

Finding Closure

In the small town of Millstone, the disappearance of key witness Sophia Jennings sent shockwaves through a community already rife with secrets. For years, she had been the linchpin in a high-profile trial regarding a series of cold cases, and her sudden vanishing left both investigators and the public grappling with unanswered questions. As her family mourned the loss of a loved one, the police delved deeper into the shadows of Millstone, uncovering a tapestry of conspiracy theories intertwined with the town's history. The stakes grew higher as the investigation revealed connections that many had assumed were buried long ago.

Detective Mark Thompson, a seasoned investigator with a knack for piecing together intricate puzzles, took on the case, determined to find closure for Sophia's family. He conducted interviews with townsfolk, each with their own version of events and hidden motives. Mark's relentless pursuit of truth led him to hidden passages of the town's past, where whispers of betrayal and corruption echoed. The closer he got to the truth, the more he felt the weight of the town's collective silence, a silence that hinted at a deeper conspiracy that could shake the very foundation of Millstone.

As Mark sifted through forensic evidence, he uncovered links to a witness protection program that had been utilized by several residents, including Sophia. This revelation opened a floodgate of possibilities, suggesting that Sophia had not simply vanished, but had perhaps been forced to. The implications of this theory spiraled into a web of fear and mistrust, as long-buried secrets began to surface. Each piece of evidence hinted at a carefully orchestrated plan to eliminate those who stood in the way of powerful interests.

The investigation took a dark turn when Mark realized that Sophia's disappearance was not an isolated incident but part of a larger narrative involving missing persons and unresolved cases that had plagued the town for decades. He began to understand that closure was not just about finding Sophia; it was about unraveling the truth hidden beneath layers of deception. With each twist and turn, the stakes escalated, leading him to question the loyalties of those he thought he could trust.

In the final confrontation, the truth came to light, revealing the lengths to which individuals would go to protect their secrets. As Sophia's fate hung in the balance, the community was forced to reckon with its past. Mark's relentless search for closure not only aimed to bring justice to Sophia's family but also to liberate Millstone from the chains of its own history. In this thrilling conclusion, the line between witness and victim blurred, leaving readers pondering the true cost of silence in a world where some truths are worth dying for. It's a beautiful day

Author Richard Trillion Mantey

Author Biography

Richard Trillion Mantey is a storyteller and writer who focuses on creating thought-provoking narratives that explore the intersection of human psychology, mystery, and resilience.

His work often examines the hidden layers of human behavior—how secrets shape communities, how truth can transform lives, and how ordinary people find extraordinary strength when faced with difficult choices.

Drawing inspiration from real-world investigative themes, psychology, and the emotional complexity of human relationships, Mantey's stories blend suspense with insight. His writing style is known for combining compelling storytelling with deeper reflections on truth, justice, and personal courage.

Through his books, he aims to create stories that are not only entertaining but also meaningful—stories that stay with readers long after the final page.

\When he is not writing, Richard enjoys studying human behavior, exploring timeless storytelling traditions, and developing new ideas that challenge readers to think more deeply about the world around them.

The Witness Who Disappeared continues his exploration of mystery, truth, and the powerful consequences of silence.